SUPERMAN
RETURNS ™

Be A Hero

by Brent Sudduth

Illustrated by John Paul Leon and Tommy Lee Edwards
Color by Melissa Edwards

Superman created by Jerry Siegel and Joe Shuster

Visit DC Comics at www.dckids.com.

First edition. Printed in the USA.
All Rights Reserved.
ISBN: 0-696-22904-8
We welcome your comments and suggestions. Write to us at:
Meredith Books, Children's Books,
1716 Locust St., Des Moines,
IA 50309-3023.

meredithbooks.com

Five years ago, Superman vanished. No one knew where he had gone or what had happened—Superman was simply gone, and the world missed him!

Superman had left to see if his home planet, Krypton, had survived the explosion he was told had destroyed it. Sadly, it had not.

Superman returned to Earth and settled back into life in Metropolis as Clark Kent, reporter for the *Daily Planet*.

"Hey, Jimmy! How's the *Daily Planet*'s best photographer doing?" asked Clark.

"Hi, Mr. Kent! Welcome back!" said Jimmy Olsen.

"Thanks, Jimmy!" Clark said. "It's great to be back!"

"Help! Somebody, help me!" Using his superhearing, Clark could hear someone in trouble.

"Oh, no!" Clark said aloud.

"What's wrong, Mr. Kent?" asked Jimmy, but Clark was gone.

Moving faster than anyone could see, Clark changed his clothes. This was a job—for Superman!

On the other side of Metropolis, the city's tallest building was burning!

"Help!" cried a man dangling dangerously from a window.

"I have you," Superman said, as he lifted the man onto the fire ladder. "Get everyone away from the building," he said to a firefighter.

Superman backed up and took a deep breath. In one amazing burst, he used his superbreath to blow the fire out like a birthday candle!

Into the sky Superman soared, all the while using his super-vision to scan the world for trouble.

A thousand miles away at the Hoover Dam, two men climbed a steep wall, spraypainting it with graffiti.

"Is something wrong with the elevator, gentlemen?" Superman joked, as he stood on the wall of the dam.

"It's Superman! Quick!" But before they could spray any more paint, Superman's heat vision melted the cans.

Superman grabbed the pair by their ankles and brought them to the police.

"Officers, please arrest these men," Superman said.

"Superman! You're back!" said the officer.

"Yes I am, officer. Please excuse me," Superman said politely, as he flew toward the Pacific Ocean.

On the island of Palau, a volcano erupted, blowing ash and rock into the sky. Lava flowed toward the city, burning everything in its path. WHOOSH! Superman sped to the tiny island.

He dove into the ground right in front of the river of molten lava. Ripping through ground and rock, he dug a trench at superspeed. The lava poured into the trench and then safely into the ocean. Who needed help next?

A team of scientists, exhausted from a hard day's work, was heading to their camp to get warm when, RUMBLE! CRACK! BOOM! The ice shattered beneath their feet, and they all began to slip into the bitterly cold waters!

Faster than the blink of an eye, Superman caught the men and flew them to safety.

"Is everyone okay?" Superman asked.

"Thanks to you, Superman!" the cheering scientists said.

In the clear, blue ocean not far from Tahiti, two scuba divers raced back to their boat, as a great white shark chased them. Its massive jaws opened, and CLAAANG!!

"Not today, big boy," said Superman, as the shark's jaws bit down on his arm. "Now, go find some fish to eat."

In the Caribbean Sea a cruise ship was caught in a monstrous storm and was about to sink. Waves as tall as skyscrapers were crashing down on the decks. Superman dove into the churning waters, lifted the massive ship, and carried it to safety.

High above Italy, a skydiving team was attempting one of the most difficult stunts when—ZIP! RIP! WHIP! Their parachutes didn't open!

The Man of Steel swooped in and caught them and set them down safely!

"*Grazie*, Superman!" they shouted, as he flew off to help others.

A massive wildfire roared across the African plains. Terrified animals ran, but the raging fire moved faster.

Superman spun his body like a top over the surface of a nearby lake, lifting the water like a tornado. Then he dumped it onto the fire. The water instantly put the fire out.

At Micro Labs in Australia, scientists raced to find a way to save lost micronauts. The scientists had been experimenting with shrinking humans, and the micronauts had disappeared. Using his microscopic vision, Superman found the tiny crew and guided them to safety.

A swim team was training at Metropolis Lake. The moment they heard thunder, the team quickly swam for land. FLASH!! A lightning bolt shot down! Superman flew between the storm and the swim team. The bolt of lightning slammed into his chest!

"Hurry to the shelter, everyone!" Superman shouted.

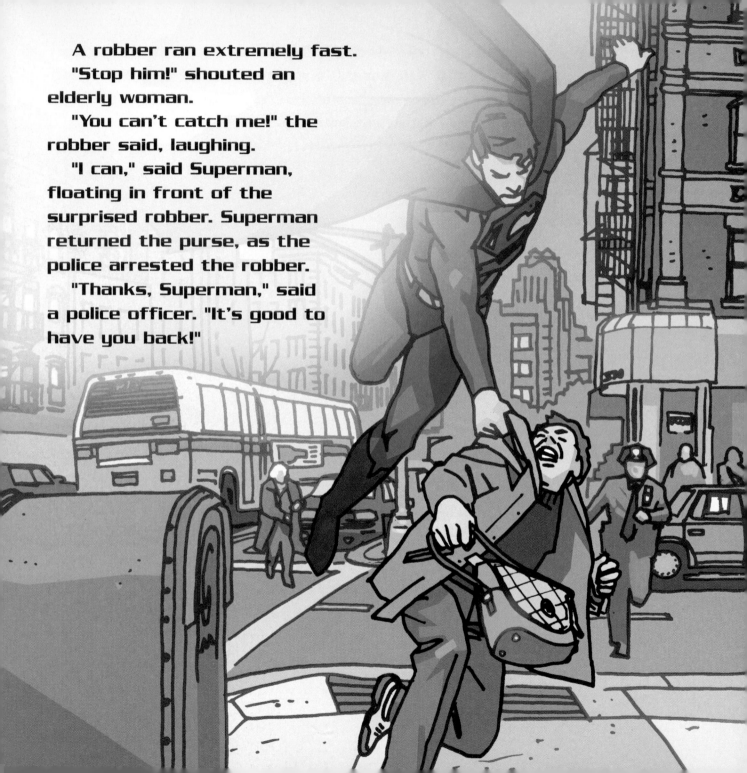

A robber ran extremely fast.

"Stop him!" shouted an elderly woman.

"You can't catch me!" the robber said, laughing.

"I can," said Superman, floating in front of the surprised robber. Superman returned the purse, as the police arrested the robber.

"Thanks, Superman," said a police officer. "It's good to have you back!"

A group of boys was playing the best game of kickball ever! The score was close, the bases were loaded, and the last player came up to kick. POP! The ball shot high over the heads of the players. Out in right field, Tommy ran as fast as he could to catch it.

The ball flew out of the park and into the street. Tommy ran to grab it.

"Careful," said a voice, as Tommy was lifted above an oncoming car. "It's safer to play in the park."

Tommy looked up to see Superman holding him.

"Wow! Thanks, Superman," Tommy said, grinning from ear to ear.

As the day was ending, Superman soared above Metropolis, zigzagging through the skyscrapers. He listened with his superhearing, but all he heard was a city that was safe and happy.

"It's good to be home," Superman thought. "It's been a perfect first day."

SUPERMAN
RETURNS™

AVAILABLE
WHERE QUALITY
BOOKS ARE SOLD.

THE LAST SON
OF KRYPTON

EARTHQUAKE
IN METROPOLIS!

COMING
HOME

I AM SUPERMAN!

BE A HERO!